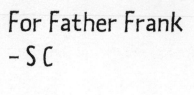

For Father Frank
– S C

For Haider Bahrani
– T M

tiger tales
an imprint of ME Media, LLC
5 River Road, Suite 128, Wilton, CT 06897
Published in the United States 2013
Originally published in Great Britain 2013
by Little Tiger Press
Text copyright © 2013 Little Tiger Press
Illustrations copyright © 2013 Tina Macnaughton
CIP data is available
ISBN-13: 978-1-58925-129-8
ISBN-10: 1-58925-129-6
Printed in China
LTP/1800/0511/0912

For more insight and activities,
visit us at www.tigertalesbooks.com

What a Wonderful World!

By Suzanne Chiew

Illustrated by Tina Macnaughton

tiger tales

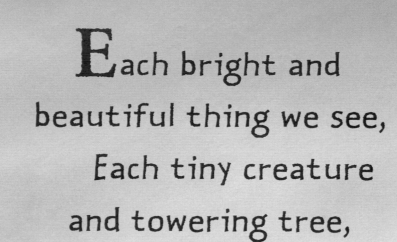

Each bright and
beautiful thing we see,
Each tiny creature
and towering tree,

Was made with gentle
love and care
And placed on earth
for us to share.

And as we see these
wonderful things,
We thank you, Lord,
for the joy each brings.

Each special day
brings something new.
Each thrilling sight,
a gift from You!

The sunny days
we spend together
Are filled with love
that lasts forever.

They make us glad
for each sweet thing,
Each precious flower
and song we sing.

The ocean, where we
splash and dive,
Fills us with joy
to be alive.

In quiet moments
that we share,
We like to stop
and say a prayer

Of thanks for every
hidden treasure,
The simple things that
bring us pleasure.

From way down low . . .

to right up high,
where rainbows
stretch across the sky,

We see new wonders
great and small,
And know that You,
Lord, made them all.

We jump in leaves
of red and gold,
When frosty days
make us feel cold.

We thank You for
new friends we meet,
Our safe, warm homes,
the food we eat.

And as our world
turns wintery white,
With sparkling flakes
of snow so bright,

We'll see Your beauty
and Your grace
In every quiet,
peaceful place.

We'll thank you, Lord,
for all You give . . .

for this wonderful world
in which we live.

We'll gaze up
at the stars above
And give to You,
oh Lord, our love.